CW00747077

THE WATERFOWL ARE DRUNK!

KATE LISTON-MILLS

COPYRIGHT INFO

Spineless Wonders
PO Box 220 STRAWBERRY HILLS
New South Wales, Australia, 2012
shortaustralianstories.com.au

First published by Spineless Wonders 2016

Cover and book design by Gert Geyer.
Edited by Bridget Lutherborrow. Copyediting and proofreading by Bronwyn Mehan and Jess Magrath.

Typeset in Adobe Garamond Pro
Printed and bound by Lightning Source Australia

The Waterfowl Are Drunk!/ Kate Liston-Mills
2nd ed.
Paperback ISBN 978-1-925052-28-2
Ebook ISBN 978-1-925052-19-0

DEDICATION

For Netty

This project has been assisted by the Australian Government through the Australia Council, its arts funding and advisory body.

BIOGRAPHIES

KATE LISTON-MILLS lives in Pambula and works as a writer, librarian and teacher. Her creative works have been published in *TIDE*, *Prowlings*, *Writer's Edit* anthologies *Kindling I*, *II* and *III* and The South Coast Writer's Centre anthology, *Seeking Horizons*. Her journalism has been published in regional Fairfax newspapers, and *Indulge* magazine features in the Daily Telegraph and The Sydney Morning Herald. *The Waterfowl Are Drunk!* is her first major creative work.

GERT GEYER splits her time between Brisbane and Melbourne, and her interest between writing and art. Previous work includes large scale murals, public art and textile design.

CONTENTS

grey. Two wood ducks swim around the spike-rushes. The spike-rushes are their home. Little puffs of feathers can be seen paddling around behind the two adult ducks; there are five ducklings all up. Every now and then a parent comes and rounds the ducklings up to deliver a lesson in diving down for food. Their little faces surface confused and wet.

In the centre of the waterhole on top of a large mound of dirt and foliage, a black swan is keeping her eggs warm. They are yet to crack. But they're close. She has named them all. She has planted her glittering hopes on each shell. Her long neck bends down every few moments to tuck in her plume. This centre mound is the swan's home and the rushes have been bowed to make a nest. The swans look like kings sitting there among the foliage in the middle of everything. The strained bellows of cows being herded up for branding puncture the swollen air of the wetlands. Some Friesians have snuck out through a fallen barbed wire fence and are scooting up the Princes Highway. The fox is momentarily distracted.

The mother swan feels the bumps of a shell moving and calls her mate. They hustle together over the mound, waiting, staring at the little chips now showing in the top of the eggs. The parents shade the birthing birds as the sun beats down. The cygnets' eyes, not yet open, are glued with fluid. And through the flurry of feathers and calls, the cygnets plop out of the eggs and sog up the earth. *Croak, croaakk, croak.*

The cows disappear into scrub. The fox can be seen clearly now, his feet well underwater. His tail is like its own creature, bushy and drenched, bobbing through like a rat. Downtrodden rockweed and pigface give him stepping spots here and there. It's quiet as he crouches in the long grass. The fox's red hair is almost camouflaged in the dry bushes and sunset. As the fox nears, the black male swan raises his head and his red beak unlocks as if silently screaming. The ducks are watching, drifting in and out of the ribbon weed. There's not much they can do as the fox picks up his pace. Their quacks, almost inaudible, are strained. They are already grieving. They herd up their ducklings and waddle towards the fence. One by one they help their little ones up onto the fence out of danger. The fox is running very fast now and the female swan lets out an excruciating cry. Her feathers are falling. One little cygnet has forced open its eyes and is searching for its mother's face. Their eyes meet for a brief second. The waterfowl and ducks shriek from the fence at the fox as he snaps at the swans and devours all four baby birds. The day is dying. The orange ruddiness of the sky pulls a blanket over the feeding fox sitting on top of the foliage. Everything is orange.

The swans are hysterical. There's a black flurry of feathers covering the mound. But they can do very little. The fox's teeth gnash and crack the shells and tiny bones. Such a long crackling chew: snaps of wing and skull. The female swan doesn't know herself. Since laying, she's forgotten. She was her children. If only she had human hands to pick them up and hold them high and out of reach. The things she could do with human hands. But it's too late now. The black swans stretch out their long wings and fly away, high into the sky's blackened sarcophagus. The blood is bright against the earth, with the dregs blowing out into the water, where the birds would all swim. The swans will be back but not right now.

The fox, high on protein, returns to where he came from. He doesn't belong anywhere, prowling continually around these butchered bogs. He flounders away, spittle lining his chops like glycerine, bits of hot bitumen melting to his paws. *Crooak, crooak.*

Everyone in the wetlands witnessed the killing. The damage drills down into their feathered bodies and wedges into their souls. Though they'd never spoken with the swans, the ducks feel the gaping hole in their family like it's their own. Their commonalities had always been more apparent: their home, their love of the wetland, their devotion to family, but now they feel their differences more than anything, like an eel has bitten off their own feet and they can no longer walk. In the bigger swamps and dams life can go on; birds continue breeding, feeding, swimming, with just the immediate family left reeling. Here in Pambula's wetlands everything stops. And the baby swans are grieved over many weeks, sometimes years. The water grows dull and the stars don't shine, they are just matte dots suspended in the black. There are unavoidable connections here, as if the swans are tied with twine to the ducks, as if the ducks are tied with twine to the waterfowl and the waterfowl are tied with twine to the magpies and the egrets and the geese and the cranes and the swallows and the wrens.

Three waterfowl are still sitting on the fence. There's a wriggling red worm in the soil below but they're too frightened to get it. The ducklings are swimming very closely to their parents. They do not wander. The diving lessons are over. The day passes. Life can almost completely fly away. But the swans will always come back. Twine is deceivingly strong.

In the sun battered streets of Pambula, stray cats loiter near the fence lines. Smoke whirls over the roofs and leaf litter gathers in the gutters. A sharp wind blows around the town's streets, carrying the aftershock of war and soiled youth. The town is still dirty with fear. It's aching for good news.

Shoals of freesias on the lawn shiver in the gust and their sugary scent moseys in through the opened windows.

Ed feels the day approach and levers himself out of bed.

Hazel, heavy with pregnancy, doesn't stir. She's struggled since Ed got the Ingleburn job. She has sweated many a night out alone with bed sheets clinging to her bits and a pesky collection of flies dallying above her head. She hates that the war has ended and yet still, Ed is only getting five-day-leave passes. Why do they still need to train youngins for war when it's over? It is over. It isn't going to happen again, she's sure.

When she stirs her boiling fruit for jam, cradling her melon-belly, she thinks about all the children her and Ed will have and how they will never have to see war. Never feel the crook chill that comes off the seas, like icebox air, freezing the beautest of days.

Lately, her sleep's been deep. Ed is home.

From the doorway, Ed watches Hazel stretch out her limbs. Her belly mountain rises like a precious monument in the sheets. He's missed her rosy smell and fingers that wear a milky coat from skimming cream. He's missed the mint sauce, stewed fruit, jam smells in the kitchen and the joy of using a clean outhouse. He's missed his Toalla Street and his mates.

Ed paces the kitchen lino and spins the radio knob. He lifts the butter-dish lid and finds Hazel's freshly made block. He spreads the yellow cream on bread and eats it, listening. The cricket is on. It's the big game. The radio commentator doesn't take a breath and the speed of it all makes Ed eat his bread and butter without really chewing.

'Miller's changing the game and Bradman wants no such thing. He's bashing that ball with more than a bat. With gumption, with fire, I tell you. And he hits! Bradman's on fire ladies and gentlemen! Fire!'

A lump of bread sits uncomfortably in Ed's throat as the punting vibes start jumping through him in currents. He needs to see his mate Bundy. They need to place some bets.

He rings the telephone exchange and the lass puts him through. Bundy is there within the hour. He clatters up the street in his old flat-trayed truck. He sees Archer Baker on the curb, the boy with problems.

The Baker family live next door to Hazel and Ed. Dick is the town's bookmaker. His daughter is about twenty-two: Ivy.

Rumours used to swirl like marble sponge but the truth was, when she was 15, Ivy got pregnant. With no partner. Some chit-chatters say she got frisky behind the Post Office just before Christmas in 1939 with Golden-Bob's nephew from Bemboka. Hazel believes a visiting soldier raped Ivy. Regardless, the town ate the scandal like a saveloy and Ivy was branded a little whore. Ivy was foolishly young and her son was a *retard* and no one in the town wanted to live next to *the retard*. Dickie had no choice but to keep her and the kid at home with him.

Ivy's boy Archer is still different, with not a proper rolling marble in his brain, they say. Ivy grieves in clumsy crocheting, quilting, forget-me-knots and jam-drops, and she never shows herself in town. She watches Archer like a bee. Fragile, but always ready to sting. One Easter during an unforgettable tantrum, he burnt the

house down by pushing over Dick's kerosene lamp.
ted blisters into the skin of Dick's left leg and killed
Rufus.

Despite their differences, the Baker trio gives Toalla Street an extra candlelight in a window and an extra friend to call when Hazel is missing Ed. Dickie gives the town something to chinwag about. And a chance to punt!

Spanners and bolts, which Bundy's forgotten, scatter off the sides of the ute and bounce onto the road. He pulls up just in front of Ed and Hazel's house, his tyres squashing the newly blooming freesias.

'I smell me a storm!' Bundy shouts from the front yard. Archer is drawing pictures on his nude body with jam. Bundy can't quite make it out. He yells out an 'Ahoy, Archie!' but it goes unnoticed. As he clambers out of the old truck he notices some of his tools strewn across the road.

Ed's Friesian cow, Gig, wanders up to the side gate to sniff Bundy out.

Bundy limps over to Gig and rubs her muzzle. He lets Gig lick the salt from his fingers.

Ed examines Bundy's limp. It looks like it's worsening. Gangrene entered Bundy's leg a few years ago and he refuses to have the leg taken off.

Then the sky rips, a long tear that neither men really seem to notice. Bundy feels some rain spatter on his forehead. He brushes it away as if it's a fly.

The two men trundle the spitting truck up to the Top Pub to sink some cold beers and place some bets. They could walk but they're on holidays. The men around town have all placed bets on the arrival date of Hazel and Ed's baby, the sex of the baby, the weight of it. They've placed bets on the storm. There isn't much that doesn't have odds on its head round here.

'Where's Dickie?' Bundy yells around the room.

'B-blown buddy if I kn-now!' Golden-Bob stutters over his Tooheys and then turns to the crowd, 'H-hey! An-nyone in 'ere kn-now 'ow to make b-books?'

The crowd goes quiet, shuffles feet, clinks glasses, whispers. The publican ups the volume on the radio and puts out some fresh peanuts.

Bundy turns to Ed.

'Eddie – think we betta' check.'

Hazel wipes the sink down with the tea towel. Flies copulate on the sill. She wonders how long they live for. How they deliver. As she fills the sugar bowl, a seismic spasm rocks her lower body and she sinks down the cupboards to the lino. A growl purges out her mouth. Again. She yells and grunts from the floor. Her grandmother's sugar bowl cracks in her hand. She tastes sweetness and sweat before another surge hits. Another cry.

Ivy hears Hazel. She hears Gig start mooing. The two bellows mingle and Ivy runs over in her thin nightie, barefooted, unaided.

The men stop in at the Bottom Pub just to whet their palate and make sure Dickie isn't in there.

'The schooners here are bigger don't you reckon Bundy?' Ed measures the glass with his hand, thumb to pinkie.

'I bloody dooo,' he cries and then tries to remember what he paid. Greyness drizzles in through the windows and off-cauliflower clouds congest in the sky. Rain is in the air. Rumbles simmer through the drunkenness and are ignored.

Several beers and a few peanuts in, the radio is switched on.

'Settle down boys! It's started!' Crowds gather into a similar scene as before.

'Where the hell is Dickie?'

Ed and Bundy shit themselves. They had been on a mission. The tipsy men bumble out to the ute. The sky has accrued an eight-o'clock-darkness. Trees are roaring in the wind, alive with the hubbub. The truck's tyres are rim-bare and skid in the dirt. They keep skidding, dirt flying out the back.

'Needsom' weight Eddie.' Ed climbs up into the tray and positions himself over the problem to give traction. The truck lugs over the sandy patch and off up the hill. Halfway up the Hospital Hill they make out a small figure running. Looks like Archer.

'Bundy, just pull over.' Ed feels hot drilling over his heart. He knows something's amiss. He should have stayed with Hazel when she was so close. Archer's running his naked, eight-year-old frame down the hill. He has one sandal on. Jam is scribbled over his privates and chest. He is yelling so hard his face is red in the rain. Ed has never seen him so frantic.

'Dick's dead, Dick's dead, Dick's dead, Dick's dead, Dick's dead,' he bangs on the bonnet of the truck, 'Dick's dead, Dick's dead…' Archer continues, gradually moving around the truck and into the gutter to let the men pass.

Bundy does a hill-start and presses his foot flat. Ed jumps off the tray and runs towards the house.

'Bad bloody day for a beer.'

Archer runs in circles around the road, 'Dick's dead, Dick's dead, Dick's dead…'

Bundy is slow to hit the brakes and careers through the cow fence. Gig doesn't budge from her position and licks the window with her long tongue – slow, cud-filled strokes. Bundy tries to clamber across to the other side and has trouble moving his leg. Ed runs into the Baker's.

'Dick? Dick? Mate, you here? Dick?' Each room is vacant. Smells of strawberry jam loiter in the kitchen. Ivy's crocheting attempt at a waratah rests on the settee, needle and thread spread across the dirt floor. She is not here.

'Must have left in a hurry,' Ed mumbles as he darts in and out of rooms. The back workroom smells of woodchips and sawdust, which still hang in the air. A scarred leg pokes out behind the sideboard in the far corner. A ladder hides the rest of him.

'Bundy! Bundy, shit, I've found 'im,' Ed blurts in a tizz.

Ivy washes some flannels in cold water and lays them on Hazel's forehead and nape. Others are cooling in the icebox. The radio is on to ease the nervy air; Ivy says this had helped her at the time. The cricket is on and the commentator is shrieking. The pace and pitch goad Hazel on.

Still on the kitchen floor, Hazel lies legs open. She's breathing quieter now.

'Your mouth should be as if you are whistling,' Ivy had said earlier. Hazel is propped up against the cupboards on sugar bags from the larder. It's impossible not to see it glistening everywhere through the screams: little crystals on her lips and through her hair, split bags weeping over the lino. Ivy has wrapped Hazel's cut hand in cheesecloth. The sugar bowl still lies in two pieces.

The ladder gets thrown across the room. Ed looks down at Dick. His white flannel is bloodless and his head is turned to the side. He is facedown. A rusted handsaw sleeps next to him.

'Dick? Mate?' Ed shakes his back. The shake starts off lightly but then grows violent. 'Dickie!' He picks Dick up by the flannel, turns him and looks at his front. Sawdust saunters over his skin and flicks to the ground. Dick's chest hair frizzles like gauze. It is still warm but his limbs are almost cold.

Bundy staggers through the doorway, 'Shit! Dick?'

'He's well dead, Bund.'

Bundy whips his hat off and holds it over his chest. The two men don't say anything for a minute or two. Dick's singlet is torn and dirty and his old body lies there somehow comfortably on the dirt floor. A hard life is hard right through, Ed thinks, and then breaks the silence.

'Better get him up to the morgue…'

Bundy grabs one of Ivy's patchwork quilts to wrap him with and the men swing Dick's arms over their necks and carry him as a wounded soldier to the truck.

Dick is laid out like a star in the tray. The patchwork is underneath him. Sooty clouds growl at each other and shoot rain down in needles. They smash on the bonnet.

The truck moves in spurts. Dick's body jumps and slides around the wet tray.

Archer sends leaf boats down the gutter-rivers. The water starts rushing faster. Archer runs after the boats still chanting, 'Dick's dead, Dick's dead,' but it sounds almost melodic now.

Gig starts wandering the streets, eating Mrs Daley's expensive tiger lilies.

Hazel starts pushing. Every shop in town can hear her yells now. People sitting in the Pambula Talkies can even hear her yells.

The men turn up the Hospital Road and Ed turns around to check Dick's still on back. Dick had been a great mate to him through the years and if this was his last salute then he was going to do a damn good job in return.

'He's moved around a bit but he's still there.'

They start talking about the game. About whether Bradman and Miller can sort it out. The rain's so heavy now they can't see the road. The tyres spin and it feels like they are no longer moving.

'You need some sand bags on the back Bundy, this is bloody ridiculous!'

The back tyres spin in the gravel and sink lower, almost bogged.

Finally after some gritty driving in first gear and some bum jumping in his seat Bundy moves the vehicle forward.

Conversation grows into an argument about Miller and Bradman. An argument about where the fuck the hospital and morgue turn-off is. About what killed Dickie – Archer, Ivy, God, poison, heart attack, old age…

They finally land in a grevillea bush and see the crumbled edges of the hospital.

'You're a fucking rubbish driver Bundy!'

'Well, you can bloody drive next time ya bastard. As if my stinkin' eyes were up to that – driving in a blizzard with a stinkin' bastard yellin' at me a-whole time!'

The both of them struggle out of their seats ducking the grevillea as best they can.

They both turn to the tray. And there's not a thing on it except the quilt.

'Where the fuck is Dick?'

Bundy feels the quilt with his own hand as if it can explain. The rain gets too loud for them to hear each other. They hop back inside the truck.

'Where the fuck is Dick?' Ed repeats blankly staring at the dust on the dashboard. 'Where the fuck is Dick?'

Bundy turns to Ed in an aggressive whisper, 'What if they think we killed him? Threw him in a ditch 'cause he didn't take our bets?' Bundy's world is spinning like a kaleidoscope and the beer is forcing sweat down his brow and turning his voice trill.

They begin their roll down the hill again. The bare-arse tyres are just gliding around: skating on a muddy rink.

Blood is soaking into the sugar. Ivy is crouched between Hazel's legs and it's all opening like a valve.

'Head! I can see 'im. Her? Head. It's a bloody head! Keep going Haze. I bloody see it!' Ivy spreads an old bed sheet around. The linen quickly starts soaking in the liquids. Ivy's face is red. She is yelling more now than Hazel. It is as if she's giving her second birthing. Her nightie's a mess with tamarillo red.

Hazel tries to turn over. The sugar grates her cheek. Her tears are copious, her hair is wet and crystalized on the floor. She lets out a wild bellow as she tries to push one more time. Her face shakes sweat off onto her blouse. The rain is spitting through the open window, across the sink and onto her bare thighs. The fresh smell of rain starts Hazel crying, it tickles her skin and eggs her on. She's always loved rain. Cricket commentators are arguing over the score count. Hazel tastes sugar. Ivy sees an upside down face howling, bloody.

The baby girl sloshes out into Ivy's eager fingers. She grabs it under the pits and wraps her in a clean tea towel.

'That's gotta be the best birth in 'istory Haze – rainwater on the skin, sugar-taste everywhere. Gotta be the most perfect girl I ever seen!'

Outside, the rain shower has slowed and the wind has settled to a whisper.

Ivy brings the wooden cot from the spare room to where Hazel lies and pops the new babe in. She pushes a glass of tank water into Hazel's weary hand and cleans the wet area up with linen and soap. She's bubbling. She traipses out onto the street and yells like she's never done before; her chest hurts with the noise.

'Hazel's had a giirrl! Hazel's had a baby giirrl!' Ivy cries harder than the clouds, harder than Dick's body feels now blocking the gutter at the bottom of Hospital Road.

Ed and Bundy find Dickie blocking the run-off at the bottom of the hill. Leaves and debris mount up on his side. One of Bundy's spanners rests on some leaves near his head. To the side of the body is a haggard cat, crouched and meowing, meowing, meowing.

The men peel Dick up and onto the tray. But his teeth are missing. His face is sallow with filth and grime and muck. Bruises and scratches fancify his body. The white of his flannel is sooted with mud and torn down the middle. Belly hair pokes through like mice.

'We're rubbish mates Bundy! Rubbish!' Ed picks off the mud clumps from Dick's cheeks and neck.

'Shit! We gotta find ourselves some teeth or we're dead meat!' Bundy is throwing leaves, branches, driftwood and other road matter around in a flurry. It's a jolting movement because of his dud leg. The cat straggles off, annoyed by the disturbance, still meowing.

But through the wind Ed can hear Ivy's yells. He's a bloody father! They are going to drop Dickie at the morgue toothless whether Bundy likes it or not.

'Definitely looks like a murder Eddie…' Bundy is buckling at the scene. His few tight screws are unravelling. The beer was probably the worst decision he's ever made.

Ed lies to Bundy. 'Bundy I'll come back and get the teeth. Promise. Let's just get Dickie to the morgue for now.'

As Ed sits with Dickie on the tray Bundy drives once again up that hospital hill absolutely shitting himself. He sees loads of his tools spread up and down the road. 'Bloody evidence! I'm a bloody goner…' he mumbles.

Ed wonders whether it looks like him or Hazel.

The cricket ends with Miller and Bradman joining forces to finish off their winning streak. Their team becomes known as 'The Invincibles'.

The drunken men from the pub straggle down the street to get a geezer at Eddie's new kid and place bets on the name. Golden-Bob has made himself the new bookie and has no idea what he's doing.

Ivy sits by the cot, still in her yesterday's nightie, just stroking the baby-skin over and over.

Women from around town start making presents.

Hazel sleeps in the sugar as if it's feathers, too exhausted to move.

Archer sits in the gutter outside the Top Pub, not a stitch of clothing on except for a sandal. Jam is scribbled over his parts and he has Dick's dentures in his mouth.

Archer's hands help him move the massive crowns as he sings to himself: 'Dick's dead, Dick's dead, Dicky's dead…'

JAM

HUMMING TO NORMAL

The radio is crackling and everything smells of tobacco. The news reporter's carrying on, something about blood in the water at the Melbourne Olympics. Nobody's listening. Hazel has it on so they don't miss the Queen's 3pm Christmas message. Everybody's knackered from midnight mass and no one can be stuffed cleaning up. The aftermath of Ed's pig trotter feast is now gelatinous on the sink. Flies chinwag in the corners of the trays and stick there. It's a rotten mess for another day.

Skedaddling around the Christmas tree are Ed and Hazel's daughters. They're shrieking like cockatoos, trying to trip each other over. It's mayhem among the cellophane. Ed and Hazel are just lolling on the settee, watching. Ed's smoking. The baby gum he cut down a month ago is gradually turning crunchy brown and the baubles are looking brighter and brighter against it. He stubs his fag out at the base of the tree.

Many times during the girls' game, the tree is almost knocked clean out of its pot. The youngest daughter, Lottie, isn't really part of it. She's on her back, face shiny with slobber, crumpling up cellophane. Lottie's been three for a while now. Three and can't crawl. Three and she can't say a word.

This year was Santa's best yet. A second-hand cricket bat and ball will sure be put to good use. Such items are like gold in these parts.

'And now a carol for the folks at home.' The radioman slaps on a recording of out-of-tune children singing, *Away in a Manger*. The two older girls, Nina and Sue, hum along with the radio and jig around in their hand-sewn pyjamas. The treadle sewing machine has made many outfits for the family and Hazel has been getting more creative as the years go by. She tries to help Lottie upright but Lottie can't hold her head up. Her legs are rockets, kicking madly, but her head sags to the side. Ed picks her up and holds her on his lap, 'Hello poppet, hello Lottie, little poppet.' He rubs her belly and she gurgles. Turning to Hazel, he lowers his voice, 'I've booked us in at the docs, Tuesday. We have to, Haze.' He scratches his eyebrow for no real reason, 'Is Tuesday fine?'

Hazel hears him but doesn't answer. She heads to the kitchen to clean up and the smoke hangs above Ed's head like a speech bubble.

Ivy from next door is minding Nina and Sue for the day and teaching them how to make jam. It's not an outside day; leaves and rubbish and branches are getting blown around the streets. Ed's waiting by the door, agitated, lighting fags, dragging them down and stubbing them out with his boot. Then he lights another one. Though he doesn't notice, a teeny wren chirps on the veranda railing. Its blue breast is puffed out, feathers ruffling in the wind and its tweet is lolly sweet. It sings through Ed's smoke. It sings in the blowy day, full of gales and rainbows. The song is louder than the other birds' songs and the melody is very clear and simple. It's honey in the ears. Lottie waggles her legs in the air on the bed as Hazel dresses her. The mauve seersucker is soft in her fingers and the crochet on the hems occasionally gets caught in Hazel's wedding ring.

'Haaaay-zle, come on, we're late!'

Inside, Hazel's frown is deep. A face chock full of worry. Full of creases. She blows warm air onto Lottie's face and the child squints in the gush.

'Haaaay-zzzzellllll!'

She heaves the three-year-old into her arms and plods up the hallway. She shuts the door harder than she means to and the brass doorknocker tumbles off its hinges and makes an almighty bang on the ground. Nobody wants to pick it up so it gets kicked to the side. The veranda is so gusty some rose pots have toppled over.

'I don't see a need for this Ed. Lottie's fine. I know what people are sayin'. I don't want a penny of it…' Hazel starts blowing raspberries, 'Bbbrrrr, bbbrrrrr,' and 'Bbbrr,' all over Lottie's cheeks and she erupts in giggles. Ed remains silent. 'Righto,' is all Hazel says but her face is full of thoughts. Her jaw is tight. Like a pigeon she totters off the veranda, watching her feet, and heads up towards the surgery. The bird's still singing and she almost notices it as she leaves. 'Righto.'

Gusts of wind hurt their ears as they walk. Even if they wanted to speak they wouldn't hear each other. Lottie isn't a happy camper. Her head is resting on Hazel's sleeve, snot seeping into Hazel's good wool. Lottie's sooking, bottom lip pursed outwards, tears shiny on her face, her bonnet threatening to fly off in the nor'easter. Her little hand darts out and hits Hazel on the face as they walk. More than the hits in the face, Hazel hates the stares of people in the street. She doesn't even really feel Lottie's hand on her face.

Inside the surgery it's as though there's antiseptic ointment wiped around the insides of their noses; the air stings and they both try to hold their breath. Everything seems to be made of cardboard, wonkily cut and wonkily glued. A receptionist slouches at the bench and Hazel remembers her from the bakery – Helen. Her mother used to say she made the best coffee scrolls in the whole of the Monaro.

The only thing that doesn't look like cardboard in the place are the blue hydrangeas propped up in a vase like big clouds. Hazel, nauseous, scans for a seat. There's many, too many. The day's quieter than dead winter and her stomach is a beast, roaring with emptiness. Lottie's sucking her soother and groaning, the noise is so brash the receptionist has to press the receiver hard into her head. Hazel is stressed with all the sounds; she can feel her heartbeat in her throat, in her head. She can almost see it beating.

When the old doctor whistles them in Hazel doesn't make eye contact with him, she steps in looking at her T-straps, her arms wrapped around Lottie like masking tape. Ed tries to comfort her by putting his hand on her back but he's shrugged off. The air still stings of chemicals.

Sliding on his spectacles, the doctor leans closer, teetering right on the edge of his seat. 'Edward, I think you know, and have known for some time, that Lottie is... retarded.' He clears his throat and then stares straight into Hazel's face, 'Down syndrome.' He says Down syndrome as if it's Nazi rule or Black Death. Hazel's got a piercing hatred for him, pissed off at his face, his voice and his sullen, stuffy room. Her face says it all. Clinching Lottie closer, away from the stinking doctor, Hazel coughs into his air trying to contaminate it with whatever he thinks she must have. The doctor looks down at his writing pad and starts scribbling, unruffled.

In the awkward silence, Lottie drops her soother on the floor. The three adults rush to pick it up, squabbling like rats.

There's a small moth flapping around the light. Inside the plastic light fitting are the silhouettes of other moths that have crept inside and become trapped.

'Yes.' Ed clears his throat and nods, 'Yes, I knew.'

After a few moments of stares and throat clearing, Hazel shakes her head and stands, 'Rubbish! Lottie's normal... just a slow learner, that's all.' Her eyes are glazed. Ed tries to squeeze his wife's hand, but shaking, she lugs Lottie out of the room, leaving him with the mongrel doctor.

'So there's really no services here, I can't really refer you to any... To be honest, I really don't know a great deal about it...'

Hazel slams the surgery door and the place quivers like a shamrock and she just stands there for a moment catching her breath. She breathes in the fresh air, long and slow. Lottie's pulling at her hair and chewing her soother like a jelly snake and the sky looks like it's about to burst and flood the moment. She starts trudging home.

The sky dots the pavement with rain and Hazel covers Lottie's head with her hand and spies the half rainbow above the cow paddocks. But it's too wet for her to show Lottie. And besides, she's not in the mood.

Inside the family home, in the main street of Pambula, Hazel grabs Lottie's baby rug and spreads it out on the wooden floorboards. She carefully lays Lottie down on her back. The rain is pounding into the windows and dribbling in through the gaps. It's speckling the edges of the cedar sideboard, but Hazel just watches it. She covers nothing. The record player is out of the rain's reach, on top of the sideboard. Hazel crawls over to it and puts on Johnny Cash's new record, *Hey Porter, Hey Porter*. She knocks the volume up to its highest to beat the rain.

'Isn't this a great song, Lottie?' Hazel kisses her on the forehead over and over.

'Da-daa-da, da-daa-da, do-do-do-do-do-do...'

They lie ogling the roof. Rain is pooling now over the floorboards, but Hazel still won't shut the windows or cover anything up. She loves rain, the smell, the sting, the newness of it. It reminds her of her first birth, the perfect birth on the kitchen floor lying on sugar bags. Rain was spitting in through the window. While Hazel licks her lips as if the sugar is still there, Lottie is trying to move closer to her. She's mustering all her strength, wiggling and rolling and she eventually makes it to her mother's side so their arms just touch. Hazel's hand is half clenched in a fist and for the first time Lottie tries to push her little hand inside her mother's. Hazel doesn't help her at all, she's too battered and dazed and consumed by the rain. She feels the pools of water stretching closer to her and the spattering outside increase. The sound is heavy on the tin and the glass. She leaves her hand in the fist and becomes quietly aware of what Lottie is trying to do. After many grunts and dribbling, Lottie manages to fit almost all her fingers inside her mother's hand. Her thumb is wriggling outside trying to slip in. Her tongue is lolling to the side; her eyes are fixated on the hand. After quite a few minutes the thumb finally slips inside and her whole hand

is neatly scrunched inside her mother's. Lottie's exhausted and her eyes close while she recovers.

'Da-daa-da, mmm, mmmm...'

Hazel feels the tiny hand within her own. She gently squeezes it and then turns her head to the other side to let the tears stream down onto the rug.

THE WATERFOWL ARE DRUNK!

Ed died at 4.20 in the morning at Bega Hospital. It was cold in his room when he went and there was nobody there except him. His last thoughts were of his three daughters when they were kiddies, bunched around their Christmas gumtree: the two brilliant girls and his mischievous little Lottie unwrapping presents and singing.

Apparently a nurse came in at 6am with a clipboard. She felt his pulse and called the doctor. Ed would be buried in his uniform but Hazel would leave his medals in the box. She thought it would be nice to keep them for the girls. Nina and Sue could pass them on to their children, as you do. The box is placed on the kitchen table. Somewhere she'll remember.

But it's important to lie to Lottie for a while. Hazel doesn't know how to tell her. She wonders how children like her deal with death?

The house is freezing. It's still dark outside. The fireplace in the back room has gone out. There is a deteriorating glow but no real life left. The cooling coals blink in the quiet spaces. A large blowfly zooms around the lounge room in a square shape and the low buzz is all that can be heard around the house. Hazel is in the double bed by herself, mouth wide open, hair in rollers, with one leg kicking like a horse on top of the quilt. With bad dreams popping in each night with the mosquitoes, her sanity is flailing through each day. Her superstitious eyes are seeing ghosts in the

corners of the rooms, wisps of grey and wicked things. She can feel her lucky streak leaving. Every night she sits her chamber pot, like a stupid dog, under her bed. And every morning she swears it's in a different spot without her having any memory of using it.

Hazel and Ed's two daughters, Nina and Sue, left to get married and have children, as you do. And poor Ed is suffering in the hospital. The whole thing has given them all flutters in the gut. And blooming nightmares.

Lottie is in the next room. She is 17 but her mind is cocooned, sealed from certain things. Hers is a teeny box room with a single bed and a series of gaudy clowns waving in each nook. There is one clown by her bed that is soft and dressed in silky pinks and standing with a red balloon. That's her favourite. Since her sisters moved out and her Dad got sick, the balloon clown has become her best mate. They talk all the time.

The phone rings and Lottie is the first to hear. She zips out of bed as if waiting for it. Her eyes widen with every step. She picks the phone up gently like a hot cup of tea.

Hello? Hello? Is that Lottie? Lottie we need to speak with Hazel, with your Mum please. Can you wake up your Mum?

The nurse can't understand what Lottie's saying. She can't see her head nodding through the phone. Her conditioned sniffs, those little sniffs a child does when crying. Hazel wrestles the phone off Lottie and sends her to the back room. She waits panicked for Lottie to shut the door. Her throat is dryer than shelf dust and her breath's already a heave.

It was peaceful, Hazel.

The words crawl through the line into her ear. She watches the lounge room walls move in. Black ivy creeps over the ground and strangles the floorboards. Hazel hits the floor and cries silently, hands clasped over her head. And the phone swings below its cradle: *beep, beep, beep, beep*.

In the back room, Lottie has her Lottie-teapot and two of her favourite Royal Doulton cups out ready. The kettle is on. She turns the volume right up on the record player and and starts singing.

'Git wiv' 'em, c'mon, git wiv.' She sways in the corner to the music, clicking her fingers and shaking her head, 'C'mon, git wiv' 'em'.

Morning sun just squeezes in through the orange trees, through the opened window.

The last time Lottie saw her Dad, Ed, was four days ago. He had sat and listened to Johnny Cash for hours, drank multiple cups of tea, and ate many biscuits with her. This morning, she sits there at her table overlooking the clothesline and back garden and pours a cup for herself and her Dad. She talks and giggles to herself as if someone else were there. Then she drinks both cups of tea.

Hazel calls her other two daughters, Nina and Sue, and whispers into the phone. There's a sparrow perched on the pickets outside. His brown head tilts to the side and his grey chest puffs in and out. When the call is over, he flies off to another house and another. The news spreads around the town. You can see women, shawls around their heads to cover their mid-perm rollers, ducking over to the neighbours' place, and men stopping their utes in the street and winding down the windows. The news is tinkering like a mechanic, slowly tapping on each head. It's tapping into the nuts and cogs of the heart of the machine, tapping each greasy component, until the parts all work together. Tommy hears about it in the pub and he's already well sloshed. He was Ed's best mate. Mates from the war. Mates from way back. He starts walking. A kookaburra follows him, darting in and out of power lines and houses to keep up. Tommy's long pin-legs are striding forward at a whooshing speed. His blonde-grey wisps of hair are blowing backwards as he goes. The town is now in motion.

Lottie finishes her Johnny Cash and grabs two bottles of Ed's sherry and a crystal glass from the cupboard. She rests them on her mother's wicker armchair on the front porch for her mate Tommy.

Ed would always tell Lottie stories about how Tommy used to help people in the war. How he became a hero. How he deserves the very best. Lottie always puts the best crystal glass out for Tommy. Always pink, her favourite.

By the afternoon the house has seen many townsfolk drop in casseroles, stews, slices, scones, trifles, bottles of liquor, and sympathy cards. The front room is flooded with sentiments and the fridge is chockas. Nina and Sue both arrive to be with Lottie and hide her from the spiky end of truth. Lottie is hugging her favourite balloon clown so tight the balloon could crack off. Hazel watches them amble into the back room; the two slender women look drawn, high-waisted flares swooshing as they step. Lottie, a whole lot plumper than her sisters, follows them with feet turned out. The three sisters squash around Lottie's petite table drinking tea and eating Scotch Fingers. Nina and Sue have protected Lottie from nasty kids, from cars, from the stove, from arguments, from certain words and from herself their whole lives. It is their quick glances to each other Lottie notices in the silent spaces. It is the way they hold their cups. It is the way they look at her, like she's a doll. Like she's Royal Doulton. Lottie puts Adventure Island on the black and white TV. Her favourite character is Clown, played by John-Michael Howson. He's the silly one. Lottie hums and sways whenever he's onscreen, giggling at everything he does. She is rocking back and forth on the lounge singing, *hello, hello, hello, hello…* to the tune of the song. She notices Nina and Sue are watching so she holds her clown up and mimics Clown on TV. Look, Ninnie. Look, Sue. Look. She shrieks with laughter when she's finished. Sue covers her wet cheeks with her mug. The three sisters sit there watching Adventure Island for a long time. Nina and Sue eventually leave around dinnertime and Lottie wishes she had put Johnny Cash on for them.

There's a knock on the door. Hazel lets the visitor in like she has done all day, although this time she doesn't recognise the woman. She's older than Hazel, leaning on a very crooked walking stick, with an orange scarf covering her hair. Her matching trousers and shirt are bright turquoise. Her silk slippers trip on the welcome mat and the crockery Cocker Spaniel doorstop tumbles over.

Good Lord!

Her exclamation echoes around the corridor. She's like an exotic bird with a shrill squawk and it takes her a while to register who Hazel is but she does. She speaks of Ed and Tommy and the war and of Hazel bareback riding through Delegate. She speaks of Ed and her own husband as if they are still alive. Hazel frowns and stirs in her sugar for an awful long time. Her local status is obvious but her face isn't familiar. Hazel sips her tea still frowning.

The woman struggles into the spare room with her overnight bag and begins unpacking. She doesn't ask. Hazel is surprised at the intrusion, but accepts the woman is staying. Though the timing is unfortunate, Hazel will have to indulge her and ensure her time in Pambula is fabulous, as you do. Out comes the fine china. Out come the silverware and rainbow cakes. In Pambula, you have to be hospitable. You just have to. But after dinner Hazel's grief soaks her thoughts and she goes back to numbness and tears. Her eyes fix on the television, but are really looking through family photo albums: of their wedding, of Ed's mischievous little face, so manly in his uniform, so dapper. Hazel retires to bed, sick of cordiality. She lies awake counting the chips out of the wooden walls, memorising the divots in Ed's pillow, trying to smell and to not smell his scent on the sheets. She doesn't know what she wants. Everything hurts. She might not wash again. Then again, she might do nothing else but wash away his smell. Perhaps it will never leave. Perhaps it's already gone.

The visiting woman falls fast asleep in the spare room. Lottie gives her own hand a few kisses and has a brief chat with balloon clown. The clown and her decide it's been a huge day and it is time for sleep.

Black and blue waterfowl patrol the street. Their beaks are rounded and red and their feet are three-pronged and leave wet imprints on the pavement. More dishes of food and drinks have been left on Hazel's veranda. In the early hours Lottie gets up to put sherry out for Tommy and to see whether he called yesterday. He had. The visiting woman gets up and wobbles into the bath.

Hazel is hyperventilating. She stomps around her bedroom over-powdering her face. The powder is thick like Selley's putty. Hazel thinks of how Lottie would always tear the house apart when she needed just her ears cleaned or her nails cut. God help her if she was to broach a serious matter with her. Hazel is struggling to breathe so she lies down among her many pillows. She throws them to the corner, she throws the bed quilt to the corner, and she throws herself onto the bed over and over again, trying to find fresh air in her hot room. Brown powder stains every bit of the white linen. She can faintly hear Lottie asking her something, and it surprises her how much anger heats her face.

Dad home? Lottie studies Hazel's face.

No Lottie!

Hazel yells too loud. She's finished with her face and is now showering herself in white powder. The powder is just making her face even hotter. And the carpet around her is snow white. Hazel's nightie is still on. She's forgotten the order of morning. She powders her face again and stares at herself forever in the mirror. She tries again. Lottie on the other hand is clear as a crystal glass and knows the order well. It's definitely Weet-Bix time.

Hazel's sons-in-law decide that, wretched as it is, the grave needs to be dug. Warren and Roy both try to call Ed's mate, who unfortunately also happens to be the town's gravedigger, Tommy. Tommy's sister answers the phone quickly, abruptly. She says he's been missing since yesterday. Warren and Roy are stumped. They search the Top Pub. They search the Bottom Pub. They walk the streets of Pambula like a chessboard, trying to anticipate the moves of a drunken man.

And so the town searches. Their Tommy is missing. Blackening above them is a hot bitumen kind of sky; the kind Hazel believes is a sign of something wicked. The world of Pambula knows how close the two men were. Dragged each other wounded for miles. Backed each other up forever.

There's a kookaburra laughing from the power lines at the top of town. He's so booming and jovial and annoying to everybody.

Lottie is confined to her back room so nobody can spill any of the awful beans to her. She's watching the news and cutting up magazines.

The townspeople are searching for the town's drunk. Boy, did they love that man. And there were stories that'd fly. There were times when he'd get too drunk and fall over and think he was in the war again. They'd find him in the foetal position with branches and rubbish pulled over him. This time the situation is different. They fear the worst.

The woman sits, dressed like a fancy bird, and starts telling stories about Tommy. There's the snort of a tired truck starting up outside so she blasts louder.

You know, when Pete was in Turkey and they was all starving, Tommy'd sneak across enemy lines.

She blows out her insides into a stiff hanky and keeps going.

And he'd snatch 'em a chook or two to eat. Tommy always got 'em food. Got 'em fed.

Hazel drifts in and out of the conversation like a dead body in the ocean. She is not sure whether she's floating or sinking but the motion sickness is setting in. When is this visitor going to leave?

The townsfolk stay out late into the night.

Tommmyy? Tommmyy?

Lottie knows there's something wrong with Tommy. The night outside is much darker than her room. Much colder. But she can hear the tone of the women's stories, the gross hum of the town in panic. She ambles out, barefoot, onto the crispy cold grass. It spears her numb feet as she steps. The clothesline is sagging underneath the weight of linens. It's so heavy even the wind can't stir it. The clothes prop is threatening to fall. Lottie checks behind and underneath the white sheets. She looks behind the orange trees, underneath them, behind Ed's shed, inside Ed's shed, inside the washing basket; but he's not there. In the hush of night's shade, her tiny call can be heard like a bell.

Tommy? Tommy?

But the wind eventually stifles her. She crouches underneath an orange tree, frost purpling her toes, and listens to the bird laughing in the background.

Tommy?

Her nightie is catching on the bald tree and no answer follows so she gives in and returns inside. Desperate, the record player is plucked out like a plush pet and she turns Johnny Cash on at the lowest volume. Johnny Cash is everything in this bungled night and Lottie sways and clicks her fingers.

'Git wiv' 'em, c'mon, git wiv' 'em.'

Still frosty from the white grass, she trundles over to the fire. But it has carked it well and truly, cold and white. Though she's never lit a fire before she's seen her dad do it heaps of times. The local paper sits open ready to be used. *Search continues for missing dementia patient, feared dead. Police have exhausted sources.* Lottie picks it up. She can't read, but she recognises the picture, rips it out and sits it on the kitchen bench. There's a small wooden box there and Lottie, intrigued, peers inside and plays with the contents. The coldness disrupts her and she returns to the fire. Eventually, she gets it to catch by blowing on it. Ash blows back onto her face, but she has no time to wash it. It's way past her bedtime.

In the morning, the mystery woman decides to cook Hazel and Lottie a chook. She grabs the light pink sticky bird from the fridge. She scrapes off the yellow jelly pockets of fat with her fingers. She places the bird straight on a hotplate on top of the stove. Initially the skin of the bird blackens. A small trail of smoke snakes upwards towards the roof. She's wearing a nightie with a lace yolk and she's humming an old tune. Her walking stick is still in the bedroom, so she struggles to move around the kitchen. Her hands grab at things as she moves to steady herself.

Hazel, for the first time in days, has plunged face first into an unmovable sleep, with her head deep in the pillow's trench. As if someone has wedgied her through the night, her underpants and nightie are fair up her clacker. Her ghosts are nowhere to be seen and her chamber pot hasn't budged an inch. Plumes of smoke slither along the ceiling and towards their room. Lottie wakes to the stink of fire. She springs out of bed, her nightie crinkled up at her chest and her hair spiky. There's no time to fix anything. Lottie blunders towards the kitchen. The woman is hooting. Flames garnish the chook and the lace of the woman's nightie. Flames singe the table where a small bit of chook has flown and then burnt the newspaper-cutting to a cinder. A wooden box and a vase of jonquils on the edge of the table have managed to escape the blaze.

Lottie rushes to the cupboard and whips out the soup pot. She spins the tap on, but the water doesn't gush in at the speed she wants.

Aw, come on. Come on. Aw, come on.

She flings the pot over the lady and the chook and refills. Sparks have flown into Lottie's hair and singed the front strands, eyebrows and eyelashes. She douses the dying flames again and turns the hotplate off. The lady's twittering has settled and she sinks into the kitchen chair and plops her head on the table.

There's a knock on the door. Warren, Roy and Tommy can see the smoke curling out of the gaps in the front door and they smash the side window and slip in quicker than a blowie.

What in God's name… Roy yelps. Are you ok? You ok Lottie? Are you ok?

Warren pats the woman on the back. He pulls down Lottie's nightie and tries to fix her hair a bit.

The smoke makes them all cough and splutter and the men fling the windows open. Grey clouds of smoke clot around the windows and gradually cipher outwards. With gratitude, the men hug the woman and thank her for looking after Lottie.

You cooking a chook, Lottles? Without a dish?

Roy looks at Lottie, but she's only interested in Tommy. She runs squealing to him.

The mystery bird woman excuses herself and retreats to the spare room. Tommy doesn't say a word to Lottie but just holds her in his soil-stained arms. He never had a wife or kids because of the war. The men smile. And it is in these wee morning hours that Hazel wakes. She hasn't smelt the smoke or heard the din, but it doesn't take long for her to realise something's amiss. In a flurry of sheets and quilts, a tiff of panic, she whips out of bed, throwing on her dressing gown as she goes. But her hullabaloo is short lived, as she runs straight into the dirty back of Tommy. He's still grogged up and weepy. Hazel's silky tears silt up her rosy bed-cheeks. Hazel squeezes him like he's Ed and inhales grief like a garden.

Found him in the friggin' grave didn't we? It's the best damn dug grave I ever seen.

The men laugh as Hazel winces and barks at Lottie.

Lottie, quick, quick, quick! Go clean up in the bathroom, off you go.

Hazel's breathing has quickened and the men take a few steps back. They loiter near the kitchen door watching Hazel, now so aged, trembling as she cuts scones in half. She puts on her frilly pinny to shield her nightie from food stains.

She doesn't know. I'll tell her. Hazel wipes her face. But not right now. She couldn't handle it.

Roy puts his arm around the widow while she flusters around.

You shoulda seen it Haze, Eddie's grave all perfectly dug, two bottles of Eddie's sherry, one empty in Tommy's hand and the other tipped over onto the shovel.

Warren tries to explain to Hazel using his dirty hands and a very hushed voice.

So imagine this, Haze. Tommy's dead to the world in a pit of muck with a bunch of fowl on'im. Waterfowl all pecking at the sherry'n drinking it. They were off their rockers! Eddie would've gone nuts laughing.

Warren shoves a scone fair in his pie-hole and is forced to stop talking. It's a small laugh Hazel musters, but still a laugh. The bird woman tramps out of the spare bedroom, with ruffled turquoise feathers. She thanks Hazel and Lottie for the hospitality and fumbles out the front door with her overnight bag and walking stick.

Hazel, dumbfounded and relieved, giggles. After all this time, she just totters out. Lottie hears her name and scuttles out of the bathroom.

You got the waterfowl all drunk, Lottles! They was fallin' all over the place! You and that sherry... Warren trails off, stuffing in another scone.

Lottie starts skulling an invisible bottle of sherry; she holds it up as she used to see Ed do when he got back from the war. Her head is right back. Her eyes are straining to still see everyone. She's giggling and sparkly now Tommy's back.

Stop mocking, Lottie! Tommy chuckles.

He gawks down at the sootiness of her face and nightie and notices there is one of Ed's medals pinned to her chest. There are sparkles in his eyes and mud all over his face as Lottie begins making him a cup of tea.

Somewhere up the street prowls a mustering of waterfowl, blue and black in the body. Their pronged feet stalk the streets, zigzagging and tripping over, until they reach the wetlands. They can't walk straight. Some of them can't walk at all.

Lottie lugs out her ironing board from behind the door in the back room and switches the record player on. She levers the legs of the ironing board out until they lock and turns the iron on. *C'mon, git wiv' 'em.* The balloon clown starts swaying in the bedroom. He also really likes this song; it's his favourite.

The clothes basket sits on the floor near the door, heaped with clothes from the last week. Nobody has had time or energy for domestic duties over this hectic week and it's so rare for Lottie not to iron daily. Ironing comforts her. It's like drinking a cuppa.

Like eating a Scotch Finger biscuit. Like getting a hug. She starts ironing.

Lottie irons Hazel's pleated skirt and adds it to Hazel's pile. She irons one of her own dresses and plops it on Lottie's pile. Lottie picks up one of Ed's shirts, a blue linen one he used to wear to the pub. She holds it close to her face so the material brushes her cheeks and she can still smell his aftershave near the collar. There is the faintest smell of beer and Lottie giggles. After neatly folding it and sitting it on the edge of the ironing board, she shuffles to the kitchen to grab a plastic bag. She comes back and stares at the shirt for a while, just gazing at the collar and the buttons and the way it creases.

Lottie picks up the shirt, kisses it and then tucks it neatly into a plastic bag to hand on to someone who needs it. As you do.

I DON'T EVEN LIKE SCOTCH FINGERS

The bus stinks like Cheezels. The Year 7-ers have them glowing orange on each finger and are sucking them off at a slow, Monday afternoon speed. The senior girls glare from the back seat, as if just the sight will make them fat. I can smell cheese and bacon balls as well but I can't see them. My friend Karlee and me are breathing out hot air onto the window and drawing pictures real quick before they disappear. The game is to guess what the picture is before it fades. We're both pretty good drawers.

Surf's meant to be good and I have to frigging go to my Nan's house for the afternoon, I've got the shittest luck. Every time the surf's good I've got to do some crap with my family. I draw a dog pooing in a toilet on the window and Karlee guesses it straight away.

The boys are all behind us chucking food in Karlee's hair and laughing about their weekends. I can see cheese and bacon balls wobbling precariously in her frizzy ponytail. I knew I could smell cheese and bacon balls. Glad they're not doing that to me. Danny starts peeling away the sole of his shoe with his fingers. The Globe symbol is almost completely texta'd over.

'How was your weekend, Danny?' Ash mumbles through his sandwich.

'Well, Ashie, let's just say I had to wash my own sheets.'

I don't really know what he means but I'm sure it's something gross. Karlee is drawing stuff on the window and then rubbing it out just when I think I know what it is.

Danny then turns across to us and explains himself, 'Thought they'd make the washing machine preggers, if ya know what I mean.'

Karlee and I both make disgusted noises and the boys all laugh.

I feel something wet near my ear and turn. Ash passes a half-eaten sandwich through the gap in our seats, 'Pass it up,' he mumbles. Even though it's a half-eaten cheese sandwich and the Glad-Wrap is releasing little shards of cheese into my lap, I get excited that it's from Ash. I like his hair and he's a sick surfer. I pass that cheese sandwich down like it's something a lot cooler than a cheese sandwich. I can't help the smile on my face.

'Hey, Karlee, there's some shit in your hair.' I pretend I've only just seen the cheesy balls.

Karlee draws a big-breasted lady with banana earrings on the window. I think the earrings are sausages and she gets another point. It really isn't my day. Karlee whinges a little more about the fact I can't go to the beach with her. But I can't. Mum is really busy, Dad is at work and Lottie hasn't been home in two days because she's in care in Bega. Lottie has Down syndrome. She's my aunty but she's really fat, has a bowl cut and is pretty annoying. Lottie lives with my nan, Hazel, and most people think Nan looks after Lottie, but lately, 'cause of Nan's oldness, Lottie has been looking after Nan. With her away, Nan's been struggling. Why the hell it's my problem I don't know. I just want a normal family. All I ever wanted was a normal family.

The school bus stop at Pambula is one of those country bus stops that has no markings, no shelter and no sign. If you've never been to Pambula you'd think the driver had got the stop wrong. It's a craggy bit of concrete, ripped up in areas, slippery as all hell, underneath a humongous cypress pine. The branches scrape along the roof of the bus as it approaches and make a very loud and annoying scratching sound. I step off onto that familiar patch of pebbles. When I look back at the bus, Danny is chucking a brown-eye in the second last window. I stick my finger up at him but he doesn't see.

There's a long golden doorknocker on my Nana Hazel's front door. The doorknob doesn't work from the outside, so you have no choice but to wait on her doormat, knocking, knocking, for someone to answer. The volume on her TV is always at 64 because she can't hear anything under 60. When it's on the whole house vibrates with the sound. I look around to make sure nobody can see me. One day I had to break in through the front bedroom window and Billy from Year 12 saw me. Still to this day he calls me Thief: 'Hey Thief, broken into any houses lately?' 'Hey Thief, the police are onto you,' and so on. Sometimes when I'm waiting on the mat I pretend to be looking through my bag or phone so I don't look suspicious. Sometimes I wait longer than 20 minutes. Thankfully, today doesn't take that long.

'Georgie, porgie, pudding and pie! Oh, it's so lovely to see you. Your hair's so long!' She flicks the corner of the welcome mat over with her walking stick and steadies herself on the wall. The smell of old-lady sanitary items, body wash and bi-carb soda pours over me. 'I've made scones! And I bought those white biscuits you like from Louie's. Hope I've got the right ones.'

I look down at her shoes. They're ugly ones that I imagine the Queen wears, navy and squarish. Nan's feet are so squashed in there. I think it's 'cause of fluid? It looks like she's got 2 tonnes of skin and spent hours jamming it all into very small navy boxes. I wonder how blood still flows. If my Mum is late picking me up tonight, I'll kill her. I keep getting these amazing pictures in my head of the boys and Karlee all surfing, nice lefts coming in near the rocks, no weed, good size, and no matter how many Venetians and Scotch Fingers I eat the images won't go away. And the constant text messages aren't helping.

> *Georgia, shit, the surf is amazing. Seriously get down here. Sou-easter, clean, 2m-ish. Where are you?*
> REC'D 15:57 09/04/2001

'Georgie, so Nina's been telling me you're surfboard riding now. That sounds exciting. I'm dreadfully afraid of the ocean. You know, when I was a kid my Mum threw me in and told me to swim. I couldn't of course.'

Nan's crinkly hand picks up a couple of sugar cubes and plops them into her cup. Little splashes land on the saucer. I watch her reach for her favourite milk jug. She's had it since I was a kid. She's never liked any others. It's cream china with a small blue bird hand-painted on the side. The blue bird reminds me of being very young and stupid. When you're young nobody listens to you 'cause you're young and stupid and boring. But you want so badly to be heard. You want so badly for someone to listen to your crap. I remember sitting at that table so many days and nights staring at that bird wishing someone would talk to me. But adult stuff was always so much more important. Now everybody tries to talk to me, but I don't have anything to say.

I lean back into my vinyl chair and put my shoes up on the table. They're my new skate shoes. They're black, blue and white and so comfy. I lay-byed them for three months and worked my butt off at the ice-creamery for these babies. Nan lets out a biting scream.

'Aaarp, up, up… oh, oh, oooh…' She shoos my shoes off the table and tries to compose herself. 'Georgia, Georgia, you almost gave me a heart attack. You cannot put new shoes on a table. Hasn't your mother ever told you that? It's the worst luck. The absolute worst.'

Mum has probably mentioned it, but I don't listen to my Mum. I shake my head as if I've never heard such bullshit in my life. Nan hobbles over to the TV and puts Blue Heelers on. She thinks everyone who's anyone loves Blue Heelers. Lisa McCune is annoying as all hell. She'd have to be the most serious person in the world. Never cracks a smile. Wears her pants waaay too high.

"OH, THAT MAGGIE!"
BLUE HEELERS 9

I know Nan wants me to ask her more about her swimming story. She's stirring her sugar cubes and adding milk crazy slow. The deliberate pause is irritating.

'So... what happened?' I indulge her, but I decide to text Karlee while I listen.

> *Hey Karlee, Fark! Me and Nan r watching re-runs of Blue Heelers. Kill.Me.Now. What's surf like? I'm drowning in Scotch Finger biscuits. HELP ME! Many peeps out?*
> SENT 16:32 09/04/2001

'Well, I almost drowned didn't I? I got stuck in a current that dragged me right out to sea.'

'Well, you just swim sideways Nan and then in to the beach. Everybody knows that.'

'Well, I didn't know that, Georgia, and I almost drowned. I was going under, crying, yelling, flailing, life flashing before my eyes. After a while, a young man pulled me back into shore and had a fuming go at my mother. She deserved it. I never went back to the beach. I never would.' She looks at my face and tries to gauge my reaction. I look up from my phone and smile. She frowns. I obviously haven't given the right response.

'And that's why I hate the number 8. Because that's how old I was when it happened. You're lucky you got to meet waves the right way, Georgie. Fancy that, a granddaughter of mine, a surfboard rider!' I wince when she says surfboard rider. It's called a freaking surfer. I study her, grossed out, as she sucks her soggy biscuit and swallows loudly.

'So, Georgie, you're almost in Year 10 now. That's starting to get serious isn't it? Are your favourite subjects still art and English? I've heard you've been going really well with your art lessons?' Her wrinkly lips are ajar and she has that upside down 'v' frown in between her eyebrows just like my mum gets. It isn't an angry look just deeply serious. As if what she's listening to could change the world. Her head is always tilted to the side a little, that right side must be her good hearing side. A large amount of time goes by before I realize she's waiting for an answer.

'Oh. Well, yeah, I still like drawing.' I have a sip of my cold tea. 'I've been learning painting, which is ok, I guess. And I like books, so I guess I like English still.'

'Pardon? I didn't hear that last bit.'

I breathe deeply and try again. I put four sugar cubes in my tea. They don't dissolve because it's too cold.

Nan smiles. 'I always liked books too. Art, well, I was never good at art. I always wanted to be. I think artists have a good grasp on the world.' She shuffles out to put the kettle on again. Her kettle is always so loud. The second the hot plate is turned on the kettle starts whistling this very high irritating whistle.

'If I sat down to draw, say, my kettle or pan, I'd draw it how I think a kettle and a pan look, not from what I actually see. Artists see things for what they are and not what they want them to be. The way things are is very important. It's important to be realistic and not spend your time in the clouds, Georgie.' She's back in the lounge room now, fiddling with the remote. I wonder whether those square shoes cut off circulation, whether when she takes them off at night her feet explode everywhere like a big squid, spilling out everywhere on the carpet.

'Do you know what you're going to do when you grow up Georgie?'

'Nah, Nan, I just want to surf.'

Her eyes point down into her tea like she can see something else in there. Maybe she can. She sometimes sees ghosts. She tells me there's a ghost called Rose that lives in her house. Whenever something unexplained happens, she says, 'Oh, that old Rosie's at it again.'

Blue Heelers goes on again. It is an episode I've watched a ridiculous amount of times with Lottie. Whenever my family have card night, I have to sit in the lounge room and watch Blue Heelers or Burke's Backyard with Lottie all night. We eat nuts and chips. Sometimes Lottie chokes on a nut 'cause she has no teeth and I have to whack her until it comes tumbling out, wet and mushed onto the carpet. It's gross. One time, we had to take her to the hospital and the nut flew out as we drove over a speed hump and my uncle caught it in his hand. We probably shouldn't give her nuts, now I think about it. I look up at the painting above the TV. It's a watercolour painting my Aunty did of Nana Hazel and Lottie standing on the front veranda. It was about 6 years ago and Lottie would have been about 40 something. Nan has her hand covering the top part of her face from the sun and looks her usual old self. Lottie's face is tilted upwards with her eyes closed, smiling as usual. My Aunty Lou has given me painting lessons on and off for a long time. The first lesson I did with her, she said, 'Don't you paint people's features Georgie, don't worry about their colours or their structures. Just worry about how the light falls on them. What parts are highlighted and what parts are left in shade. The person comes to life once you get this right. You just worry about the light, Georgie.'

My phone beeps again. Nan's getting super sick of it.

> *GEORGIE! Where are you? Surf is cranking!*
> *Just came in for new leggy. It'll get dark*
> *soon. Hurry.* ☺
> REC'D 17:03 09/04/2001

> *Dude, I'm at my frigging Nan's. Long story but*
> *I'm pissed about it. Enjoy the surf for me.*
> *Betcha it's flat as tomorrow…*
> SENT 17:09 09/04/2001

Maggie-Harry-High-Pants, aka Lisa McCune, is on the TV carrying on trying to spoil the fun again. Nan's loving everything, saying, 'Oh that Maggie. Oh, you can rely on our Maggie.' I am getting a shit-tonne of messages. Why today? I mean I would have come in and done this any other day, but it had to be today didn't it? I seriously think I am adopted. I don't even like scones. Or

Scotch Fingers for that matter, they're super bland. Mum's late. I'll kill her. I start drawing a wave on my arm with a nearby pen to take my mind off how angry I am.

'It's so good to have you here, Georgie, I've missed you. You haven't been in in a while.' Nan fluffs her curls up around her face. I don't know why ladies all cut their hair off when they turn 50 and then spend the rest of their days perming it. Do they not know it's a pretty tragic hairstyle? If all old ladies have the same do, wouldn't you think, gee, I don't want my hair to look like every other old woman because it'll make me look old? Nope, they just all run out and do it. Sorry, waddle out and do it.

'I tell you what, Georgie, Meals on Wheels has been pretty good lately and I kept you some soup from lunch. It's chicken and corn. It's delicious, I promise.'

It's hard to keep this act up. I could think of nothing worse to eat. She knows I'm vegetarian, but she still doesn't think chicken is meat. I look at the tiny rollers in her hair. I look at her pink knitted jumper, the way it fits over her droopy boobs. It is hard to see resemblance between me and the entire family. I think it's definite; I've got to be adopted. I've got nothing in common with any of them. I watch the TV and just zone in on Lisa McCune's annoying face, her camel toe, her taut lips. Her face reflects exactly how I feel right now. Pissed off at life. Mum should be here by now. And then I'll get down there. I don't care if a shark eats me 'cause it's dark, I am going surfing. And I am not eating another damn biscuit. And then, the text that beats all others…

George. I just got out. Amazing. Where were you? –Ash
REC'D 17:23 09/04/2001

Holy shit. Ash. I re-read the message about 8 times. He called me George! That's got to be an affectionate thing to do. Although, maybe it's a friend thing to do? Maybe he doesn't like me *that* way. The fact he noticed I wasn't there is the one wicked thing to come out of this shit day.

Nan is talking about the police force. 'It must be such a difficult job. So many terrible things in the world now…'

I can hear Mum's car pull up outside. I'm finally outta here! 'Well, Nan, it's been so nice to see you, you look great, thanks for the food.' I yell it out as I jog up the hallway, pulling my schoolbag over one shoulder.

Mum comes in looking fragile and weary. She walks in and starts talking with Nan but I'm outta here. I jog past her in the hallway and she stumbles out of my way. I see a twenty-cent coin on the pavement on my way to the car. I pick it up and pocket it. That's lucky isn't it? I'm definitely gunna have a good surf now. And I'm in the car. I'm putting my Walkman earphones in. Oasis is playing my favourite song. It's that one, you know, that one that talks about Sally? You know the one. I'm on my phone. I'm wondering what board to take out. I'm sliding my swimmers on underneath my t-shirt. I'm calling Karlee. She's not answering. I'm breathing heavy. Mum finally gets in the car.

'Georgia, you didn't even say goodbye to your Nan.'

She starts up the car and takes a slow and deliberately loud breath, 'At least wave to her.' She flicks the blinker on and looks for oncoming traffic. 'I don't know who you are anymore...'

I can hear Mum talking but I'm not really listening. Oasis has me right there in that chorus.

Nnerrrr, ner, ner, ner, nerrrr...

I look at Nan's house as we drive off and I see her clutching her walking stick, waving to me with the other hand. She's standing on her veranda and the last sun of the afternoon is shining onto her face. It's like patches of golden pepper are sprinkled over her cheeks and forehead, leaving shadows underneath. And for just a second, I realise the sun falls on Nana Hazel's face the same way it falls on mine. And then we're gone.

WITHOUT FLOATIES

When he was 7, Michael Swaney's parents drove to a place called Pambula to try and salvage their vegetable-scraps-in-the-plughole-of-a-marriage. But the drive from Melbourne was longer than anything Michael could remember, especially since it had been advertised to him as a fun thing to do. To his satisfaction, the first week was indeed full of vanilla ice cream, fishing with hand reels, and beach cricket with a stick and a can of Fanta. He remembers seeing his mother and father holding hands. He remembers them laughing so hard tears came out of his mother's eyes. But in the last week things went back to normal; it all became fraught with terse words, scary fights and superficial holiday-hat wearing. On the last day, they drove to Pambula Beach one final time. His father decided Michael could 'pretty much' swim so he took Michael's floatie vest off. Michael was stoked; finally, he was a grown up. He remembers looking up at the sun on his way to the water and it was just like a big fried egg.

Michael waded in with his father, holding his hand. The sea was like diamonds on his skin and there were mounds of foam and water that came and pushed him, called waves. They were fabulous things, until one of them pulled him under. It was extremely strong. He tried to hold onto his father's hand, but he panicked and sucked in water and their hands were jimmied apart. Michael felt himself zoom around underneath the shore dump like a lost sandal or set of goggles. What felt like hours, were only seconds and then Michael's father seized him so hard that nails pierced his arm skin. The force was so ferocious Michael assumed he was in trouble for not being the good swimmer his father thought he was and for letting go. After coughing up heaps of water, Michael was shaking. His little hands tried to wipe his face of tears, sand, snot and shame but it all just stuck there. The fights on the way home were the worst ever. And it was all his fault.

Today, Michael Swaney, at the tumultuous age of 19, attends his father's funeral. There's a box of his father's things sitting in the back of his car that he never ever wants to unpack. The sky is an old punnet of blueberries. The church glows against the blue. Its stained-glass windows have Jesus dying all over them. A puny cluster of mourners dribble into the cathedral all wearing as close to black as their wardrobes could accommodate. Michael wonders if life can be judged by how many people attend your funeral. They all stand like bowed insects rubbing their spindly legs together, pretending to read the booklet. There are two speakers at the funeral, but not one funny story between them. Not a whole lot separates the two: 'He liked a bit of adventure, not one to be tied down,' and 'he was a quiet and kind man.' But there was nothing of significance, 49 years without much to say and without a legacy. In a city, really, how is anyone supposed to make an indent? But that's what Michael loves about the urban maze: the anonymity gives everyone freedom to do as they please. As Michael fidgets in the first pew he wonders what his father looks like inside the coffin, what's on his face, how's his mouth? Downturned? Disappointed? Surely. And for just a moment he regrets not going to the viewing. Maybe his mother has made it up. Maybe this is all a hoax. And even if his father is in there surely this isn't a true reflection of his 49 years.

The church pew is uncomfortable as all shit. He watches his mother. She's bejewelled: golden like a pyramid with diamantes everywhere and extremely upset. She's wearing her sunglasses inside. Michael tries to imagine what she's feeling, but he can't quite decide. Something between anger and sadness. Maybe regret. He watches her hands tremble on the back of the seat and he almost feels sorry for her. She wouldn't have ever wanted this. The priest jiggles puffing incense around the coffin like a rattle and the mustiness relaxes Michael. He thinks of the sea and how his father loved water. He thinks of the foam that blows in little bits from the tops of waves in an offshore wind. The fluffy blobs land softly on the water. Eventually the blobs float back out to sea unwanted. His father had somehow been dismantled over time. Like his mother had seen the end picture and had started removing the jigsaw pieces. The priest puts the rattle away. The church smells like an old boot and Michael tries to hold his breath.

Michael never got swimming lessons, though he asked many times. His mother said Melbourne 'didn't have any pools for swimming.' Some people might call it helicopter parenting, but Michael thought it was maybe what happens when love is so tightly wound around a balloon it changes its shape. Michael would never burst. He would just adapt. And so he is wary of water. But something always jerks him back, visualising it, clear and silver in the heat. Splashing. Calming. He can see himself in his crumpled black suit falling straight down into a deep ocean pool, feet first, tiny bubbles floating up around him.

It's right when Michael is driving from the church to the cemetery, zooming through the suburb of Narre Warren, that he swings straight onto the Monash Freeway. He doesn't think, just swivels his car around and onto the whopping road. He decides to drive to Pambula. He doesn't really know why. He's angry. He's speeding. Hot tears run and sting. He's boiling and ruddy. His old Barina clocks up 140km and the steering wheel wobbles in his hands.

On the drive up from Melbourne, he swears and screams at his windscreen, head banging to Limp Bizkit. Music is how he copes. His mother would bust his chops if she knew; she hates his music. With every hump in the road the box of his father's things clatters and Michael wonders what's in it. It's sure to be filled with junk.

When Michael Swaney drives his lolly-coloured Barina into a camping spot near a river, he notices the dead wattle trees. The grass is tawny and puckered, not fluoro like Melbourne lawns. Bracken scratches the earth, bald in places and horribly thirsty. Michael flips himself out of the car like an omelette. His bum is numb from driving so he crawls around, arching his back and limbering up, before standing. It's all the same as he remembers. Small towns don't change, they just age. There's gooey sap bleeding out of wattle trunks. A wasp nest hums in one of the canoes. The golden river is fizzy like ale. Big fish, little fish bubbling in and out and slapping down on the water. The sound echoes around the cliff face, and seems to boom back and forth throughout the rocky cathedral. Michael edges towards the BBQ to assess its cleanliness, but it's been so long unused creatures have nudged out the bricks and are nesting inside. It's rusty, boxy, and useless. He touches it gently and russet powder stains his fingers. It's the sandflies whirring around his face that make him realise the day is cooling and closing around him.

Michael sleeps on the back seat of his car. Through the night, he wakes to wombats fighting outside with their horny grunts. And the box of his father's things looking at him.

On the second day, he whizzes into town for supplies. Down the main drag stand two pubs. One up the top, called Top Pub and one down the bottom, known as Bottom Pub. This fact alone is enough to almost make Michael light a match and set fire to the streets. Why on god's earth would a town of five people need two pubs? Alcoholism, he decides. He feels like spitting on the ground.

Michael, in the distance between the bottom of the main street and the top, encounters several conversations that accentuate the supreme crappiness of small town living. One teenager has a 'fork-itching' case of thrush, now broadcast around the streets by some old fart; the supermarket's out of smokes, according to a very pissed off tradie; and there's a blue-tongue staking claim on the hairdresser steps. Women are carrying on and shooing it with shampoo bottles and a feather duster. Michael boots a Mount Franklin bottle right up to the metal newsagency sign and it makes a *ting* when it hits, loud enough to make the old codgers outside jump and grumble. All this, for some baked beans and clean water.

He hasn't driven all this way for nothing. Surely. Something decent must be here, otherwise his parents wouldn't have carried on about it. Michael phones the local national park service to see if someone can show him around. They put him onto an Aboriginal Elder named Wal. Wal is meeting him at the top of town to take him to a place called Nethercote Falls. Michael's still wearing his funeral shirt and has hatched some old shorts from the boot of his car.

Nethercote Falls is a bizarre natural formation. Michael walks around the rock pools bloated with yellow water, swelling in the sun. Clear as a jar. He can picture his father in a place like this, ripping his clothes off, and springing off any ledge. Michael tries to zone in to Wal's dawdling voice half lost in the breeze.

'And it's fresh water obviously and because it is moving, technically, you can drink it... haha, I probably wouldn't though, kids pissing everywhere...'

There are giant cliffs rising up from a river with water gushing out over the edges. Near where they're standing are giant pools that look deep enough for whales. Young people are bombing off the cliff ledges at different heights. Some hesitate. There's a girl of about 14, bobbing near the edge halfway up, squealing as her boyfriend tries to push her over the edge. The adrenalin is almost contagious, and Michael has to stop his mouth from moving up into a smile. As another gawky teen launches off the highest ledge, Michael imagines it's his father jumping. He would have loved the thrill of hitting the foam. The history, the fossilised fish and grubs and the nippy, clean air.

Wal decides to take Michael to one of the two still-standing Aboriginal fish traps in Australia. As Michael sits in Wal's car watching the dust fly up in the side rear-vision mirror he imagines what the fish trap looks like and how it could possibly be intact.

He visualises grass woven into a net formation with little hooks made out of stones and shells and strung across a river, useless and archaic. Wal eventually pulls the car over and starts wandering through thick scrub. Michael follows, but begins to wonder if Wal is taking him to some deserted murder nook.

'Um, Wal? Where are we headed?'

Wal laughs at Michael. 'Your city legs tired already? Not much more. You can already sort of see it, mate.'

Michael searches for a large net or box or cage, but all he can see are boulders, evergreen shrubs, and frothy water. Nothing out of the ordinary. Just a boring, bucolic scene.

'Can you see it?'

Michael doesn't want to say no, so he says nothing.

'It's right in front of you, Michael.'

Michael stares into Wal's face like he's crazy. It's riddled with tunnely laughter lines. His eyes are bottomless. Michael is suddenly intimidated. He tries to gauge Wal's impression of him. But all Michael sees is himself in the pupils. Wal's eyes are too deep and Michael quickly looks to his feet.

'Look at the rocks, Michael. Follow them around. Don't look just at one, watch how the water flows.'

Michael tries again. He begins at one side of the river and follows the rocks, trees and water around, melaleuca by melaleuca, until he realises the whole thing is the trap. The fish swim upriver with the tide and the rocks and boulders trap them on their way back so you could just pick them out still flipping. The formation is round like a campfire. Michael imagines people standing, waiting for their meal fifty thousand years ago. The water, trickling and gurgling, snakes through the rocks, over, under and around. The rocks are like couches sat in by the same person for donkey's years: smooth, moulded, loved. Michael breathes in the spring air and the chill of it seizes his lungs.

'Can you see it, Michael?'

Michael doesn't answer he just nods. He doesn't speak the entire way back to town. As he gets out of the car, he shakes Wal's hand

and thanks him. He gets in his own car and sits there for a long while.

It's about 2 o'clock when Michael puts on Linkin Park. His car's still sedentary in the main street of Pambula, sweat pooling on his back. The terrible mood has returned and he screeches onto the highway. He halts at Pambula's only roundabout waiting for cars to pass. What becomes clear is that there's a funeral procession on, from church to cemetery. He spies the coffin, nested like a black swan in the back of the hearse. For a second he feels his father is inside, like the tiring day has propelled him back through time to live the hell again. He finds himself imagining what his father's body looks like now caged up in the coffin, what he's wearing, what condition his skin is in. Car after car creeps after the hearse. There's traffic banked behind him for as long as he can see. He skulls some Coke from his bottle and has a sneaky pick of his nose behind the other hand and still more cars come. Michael Swaney begins to realise this dead person is not his father, but that they are, in fact, famous. Sorry, *were* famous. Every shop in the street is locked up and the staff members are standing outside the shops watching and bowing as the procession lumbers past. Michael feels hot, so he pulls over and parks. He whips out of his car and waves the bottom of his shirt around to get air circulating. He puts his head between his knees to let the blood rush down and in the sudden quiet he can make out *The Rose* being played by flutes. His mother used to play him *The Rose* on the flute when he was a kid and tell him it was the most beautiful song ever composed. He wonders if they played anything at his own father's grave. He rubs his forehead with his hand and wipes the sweat onto his shirt. There is no way in hell he can get back to the river with this procession going on. And it's too hot to get back in his car with no air conditioner.

Somewhere between *The Rose* and *Auld Lang Syne* he ambles towards the cemetery, then claims a spot at the back among the shit-tonne of people. The fact that he is standing at some old fart's graveside ceremony when he didn't even go to his own father's is making him laugh. Not a normal laugh, but a hysterical sort of giggle where his forehead is frowning but his mouth is bearing all teeth. Up near the coffin and freshly-dug hole is a girl about Michael's age who isn't in blacks like everyone else. She's wearing fluorescent orange board shorts and a pink singlet. Her hair is crazy, like blackberry bush crazy, with different coloured streaks through it. She glances at him a couple of times, trying to work out who he is. Michael quickly looks down at the grass, with a sudden woeful look on his face. The speeches are endless, the flowers too. But Michael fails to listen or see any of it. He's hooked on the girl. She's his white rabbit in a sea of mourners. Towards the end of the ceremony, she walks over to a Down syndrome lady and puts her arm around her. Michael looks away uncomfortable.

Michael waits until they all vacate to the wake for his chance to talk to her. But as he starts walking over, he realises his chance has flown as she jumps into someone's car. And maybe that's a good thing, because he didn't really know what to say anyway. Michael stays until all that's left are three oldies gathered by a faraway car chatting loudly. He gathers the confidence to move closer to the grave. He didn't view his father's body, put flowers on the coffin, or read the headstone, but now he strides right up to the grave. He's aware the funeral people will come back at some point to cover the coffin with soil, but right now there's just thousands of flowers, like a patchwork quilt stretching for many metres. He crouches down next to the headstone and expects it to say: 'His books were loved the world round,' or 'his contributions to medical research and to Australia's public health care system will endure' or 'he'll be remembered as someone who fought for justice and democracy and whose name will rest among the greats of this nation'. He honestly wonders whether the funeral was televised. Had he seen a camera there among the crowd? But all he'd really noticed was the colourful girl's presence juxtaposed against the darkness. Michael leans over to move some flowers covering the headstone and reads: *Hazel Ward – a loving wife, mother and grandmother. May Heaven have tea and biscuits Nan.* And that is all it says. Michael shuffles more of the flowers aside to try and read more, but there is no more, just a crinkly photo of her face, beaming underneath oversized reading glasses. It's hard to pinpoint what he feels, but it's probably something like betrayal. Like life was a secret he was never told. He trudges back to his car and hoons off past the droves of people walking to the wake. But she was no one. She was no one, surely.

Back at the salty river, Michael feels a hunger in his belly. His fingers fumble with the fire starter. It takes eons to catch. He stares into the coals, watching the white powder blow over the twigs and his hands. The sun is warm on his back. Even though it's a hot day, there's always a breeze blowing round here. Michael decides he should open his father's box. He grabs it from the car and sits it on the nearest log and just looks at it. Such a plain, brown cardboard box. Eventually he musters some courage and opens it. He expects there to be a whole heap of shit, but inside are his father's model boats and planes. When Michael was a kid they used to build them together and laugh when they got it wrong; these ones were all the right ones. He touches the dry wood of the hull of one of them and he feels water in his eyes. At the bottom of the box there are some old fashioned woollen vests that he's assuming were his grandfather's and an envelope with *Michael* written on the front.

The newly born flames tussle with the breeze and almost go out. He leans over and cups the flames with his hands to protect it from the wind and it finally strengthens. It starts heating the old coals. Michael lifts the pull-ring of the baked beans and oozes the contents into the frypan. He holds the pan just over the hot coals and crouches down beside them. While he waits, he opens the envelope.

DEAR
MICHAEL
MY
BOY
BEANS

Dear Michael, my boy

Strokes are shit son, so look after yourself. My nurse is bloody writing this for me because I can't even hold a pen. I want to say thank-you. Thank-you for being there for your Mum when I couldn't be. Things between us were not your fault. I never listened to your Mum and I was never the type to marry anyway. I'm a free spirit, you know that mate.

You've grown into a top man and I'm a very proud father.

My father always taught me the 4L's: Always love, listen, learn and try to leave a legacy. I have failed on most of those but I'm sure you won't.

Love Dad.

Michael's eyes remain fixed on the letter. Some of the baked beans begin to quietly explode, shooting out of the pan. Some land on his feet. The sharp stings wake him. *Fuck, fuck, fuck!* He licks the exploded beans off his arms and runs the pan towards the river. The pan yells and sizzles as he thrusts it into the yellow water. Little beans float to the surface like buoys, have a little bop and then sink down below. He's in up to his knees, bending over so his hands are also submerged, washing off the tomato sauce. A sea eagle swoops down from the cliff edge, dives into the water and comes out with a sizeable trevally in its talons. The sound of its wings hitting the surface makes Michael jump. The bird joins its mate in a bald tree nearby and Michael thinks how much his mother would have loved watching the two giants feast like kings. Michael studies the entire picture, how the water drips off the gouged rock faces, how it runs down to the river and becomes a whole. He throws the pan back onto the bank and wades over to a large, slippery trunk half submerged. There are some oysters glued to the side. Michael struggles up onto the trunk, leaving his feet submerged. Two small toadfishes swim up to his feet to sticky-beak. It's his reflection that dismantles their little bodies; a giant gangly human being, glinting in the sun, scruffy black hair camouflaged in the shadow of the weed, perched like a cormorant on the trunk. He wants to slip down into the cool river, but he's scared.

He sits there for a long time. Eventually, holding the trunk tightly, he wades in. He lowers his pale body all the way up to his chest. His legs kick behind him like a young frog and he puts his face under and opens his eyes. Underneath is clear and salty and full of fish and movement. The water gets colder the deeper down his feet go and he follows the trunk further into the river. Gradually, he lets go of the trunk and begins to swim like a little boy who's never swam before. And the yellow water pushes him upwards like the helpful hands of a parent.

SHINY LINO AND A WHISTLING KETTLE

Oh I may be right and I may be wrong
But you're gonna miss me when I'm gone
Well the engineer said before he died
There were two more drinks that he'd like to try
The doctor said what could they be
A hot cup of coffee and a cold glass of tea

– from 'Rock Island Line'

My husband is thrumming to Johnny Cash in the bedroom. He's singing really fast, anchored to the sofa, hair in coiled springs, voice low and blowy. The pace is picking up. My kettle is rattling in the dock, about to blow. The steam is cumulonimbus. Ghostly.

For as long as I can remember, my Nan used to screech out from her room, long and loud, *Lottieeeee, put the kettle on!*

Always agreeable and eager for tea, Lottie perpetually had the kettle boiling and it would just whistle forever. You'd come in to an empty house whistling. Even when you'd well left that house there'd still be whistling in your ears. Electric kettles just turn off. But I can still hear the whistling. Like steel on steel, metal flying like glitter as the machine giddies up, or comes to a halt.

I've only really started drinking tea and coffee in the last few years. Tea and coffee was what old people talked about, what old people craved, what they did. I've never felt old until recently.

Coffee was from the movies. It was that fat-free thing skinny women clutched as they ran to work in their heels. It wasn't just an excuse to get out of the office; coffee queues were the pick-up place, the flirt-fest, the dishy mid-morning catwalk, where everyone was glossy. It was the socially accepted frivolity that bristled my hairs. Coffee tastes like shit. When I moved to the city, I used to drink mochas to look like a real adult, but I could still taste the coffee; it was like a Warhead covered in chocolate. When I turned 27, I realised I was practically an adult, or pretty damn close, so my tastes needed to mature. I'd realised pretending to like coffee was rather lame so I started drinking tea, hard core. I was peppermint and jasmine petals. I was ginkgo biloba. With each sip I felt older, like your first drag of a ciggie, or your first spin in a car, and it wasn't long before I woke up feeling ancient. You see, there's a very gaunt line between young and old. Sneeze and you'll miss it.

When I watched my aunty Lottie die I was fuelled up on chilly tea. I was icy English breakfast. The kettle had long gone cold.

As I pour the steaming water in, the tag bobs from side to side threatening to fall in. Sometimes when it does fall in, it separates from the string in the heat and floats to the bottom of the cup.

Fuck.

Then you have to dirty a spoon getting it out. I've always hated washing up. Lottie loved it. And she loved drinking tea. I'll always remember her swaying on the glistening lino floor, with her fingers dancing above her head, waiting for that kettle to boil.

Aw, come on, come on. Aw, come on.

The first few moments she'd twirl and fuss about the kitchen waiting for the whistle. Down a few bickies in excitement. But the last few moments when the metal cap on the spout was quivering in the steam, not yet blowing, she'd curse and carry on. She was toothless and gummy. Round like a float and dumpy like a sponge cake. Hot water was a temptress for her and her cup. She'd dunk the bickie in, make it soft and swallow it whole.

I remember when I was a teenager and started having sex, I remember saying to my mum, if I ever found out I was pregnant, and it was Down syndrome, I'd abort it. I'd been around disability too much. I get why my mum cried like a cloud and walloped her bedroom door hard against the socket. She walloped it three times, because Dad's hat was hanging on the corner and stopped it fully slamming. It fell off by the third time and she got the slam she wanted.

My aunty, Lottie, had Down syndrome. Kids got scared of her in the street. So she never looked at people when she was out. Until I left school, I was always too embarrassed to associate with her in public anyway, you know except for family events. I'd just die if anyone at school knew. But since leaving school I'd started to walk past her in the street and try to catch her attention.

Hey, Lottie! You doing some shopping? Hey Lottie? Lottieeee?

But she'd never answer. Her nurse would encourage her to look up at me but I guess it was too late or something. Teenage dullards used to call her a retard. They used to scream it in her face when she was young and by herself, so she learned to go into autopilot once she left the front door.

My husband has moved on to Jackson. Always a favourite.

I remember my aunty Lottie swaying to Johnny Cash in the bedroom. I'll always see her in that back room, skirt billowing in the movement, hands silently clicking. Those old lady skirts chosen by Nan. She thought they were feminine and flash. Lottie never argued, she just wanted everyone happy. Dedicated tea drinkers like peace. I put the kettle on again. The steam and ghosts can reconvene.

Apparently, this house is haunted. The family struggled to sell once Nan died, so it fell into my lot. Penniless, I became a home-owner, engulfed with debt and ghosts – but I was one of the lucky ones. I look down at the shiny lino and think of Lottie standing here looking at her feet. She used to love shoes. Her funky pink slippers would slip along the lino and make the covering of blowflies scatter in the heat. For some reason blowies used to love crawling on the floor here, probably because Lottie would spill all kinds of gooey goods down there daily. The blowies would blend in with the pattern, add to the sheen, and Lottie wouldn't even know what they were, they were just part of the kitchen. Black dotty ground it was, blackened, chipped lino it still is, and if I had the money I'd rip it straight up. The lino is like butter beneath my feet, it melts and softens in the heat and makes that sticky slurp when my shoe moves.

We used to have this joke, Lottie and I. We'd tell the other they had nice lippy on. Neither of us ever wore lipstick. It probably doesn't sound that funny to most, but it was humdinger to us, and it never grew old. When I got the call she'd been rushed to Canberra hospital, I hired a car and fair dinkum flew. I was falcon fast. I wet myself a little cause I just couldn't stop. Sometimes the gusts of spring wind were so ferocious the car almost blew away. The violence of it lashed my windows and I saw them bend as I turned to ice. The heater couldn't even warm me up. My knuckles whitened around the steering wheel and my eyes focused solely on the white lines, I was all about the white lines, and staying inside. When I finally drove in, Canberra was bristling with ice and tulips and intersections. After the sweet smell of Floriade, Woden was a baton that belted me silly and made me want to spew freely through the hire car. Nerves kicked in and my foot shook on the clutch. Pig-rooting like a horse, the car lurched into the car park where my sister and uncle were waiting, flannos and jeans, frizzy and tired. My sister warned me about what I was about to see. But shock couldn't be teased or groomed.

I've decided I do like Scotch Fingers. They are a superb shape for dunking, they are inoffensive in flavour and therefore suit all moods. Except my aunty Lottie can no longer ask me if I want one. She can no longer make coffee so strong your eyes almost spin off your face. I've got nobody anymore to play the lipstick joke with, and I actually – despite how I often grumbled – really loved that game. It was stock sturdy and home, smack bang in my comfort zone. You know, I actually drew on the brightest, boldest pink lipstick that day at the hospital. The first thing she said to me through her squinted eyes and cords was, *n-nice l-lippy*, followed by a weak giggle.

The giggle came out of her mouth so quiet and beautiful that I cried. The nurses, surprised at her revival, left us. My cousins arrived one by one and got similar welcomes. Life made sense again to her. Life made no sense to us. It was *our decision* the doctors said. They had no idea what was wrong with her. They were curious as to why *people like her* die earlier. Was it a protein build up 'round the heart? Were the organs just falling like dominoes?

It turned out her heart was harder than steel. All her joy had built up around it and stiffened. Her liver copped the brunt, expired, and turned her skin orange. She glowed.

I break the Scotch Finger in two, place one on the saucer and dip one in amidst the steam. In the final hour, we spoke to Lottie about eating chippies at the Pambula Milk Bar, drinking 'chinnos, Scotch Fingers and ironing shirts, of Johnny Cash, ice cream, cups of tea and washing powder. She nodded when we said tea. She'd been waiting all day for one. The simplest things can be the saddest, 'cause we all sat there looking at her pretending, lying straight to her face.

Yep, we'll eat chippies at the milk bar tomorrow.

Just before she left us, we told her she was going to see her mum. Her mouth was smiling, waiting for Mum, waiting for tea. You could hear the oxygen drop like a pin, you could feel it.

Death becomes very clinical. In a second a person turns into a body and the objects around them have to be taken away. I wish now I'd had a kettle there, just so she could have gone out to the burbles of boiling water and the smell of Lipton and biscuits. But she glowed all the same. Little pom-poms dangled from her ankle socks; those pink woollen socks slid off her dead feet like silk and I folded them into each other. They felt like tissues or feathers in my hand. Perhaps death was weightless. Only Lottie would have pom-poms at her ankles, only Lottie could paint a hospital room bright pink. I guess the little things really are the big things, because I can't remember what I thought at that moment, other than tea,

A HOT
CUP OF COFFEE
AND A COLD
GLASS
OF
TEA

chippies and Johnny Cash. She died waiting for a cuppa, even though there was no kettle boiling.

The floor of the hospital was slippery. My hands were fists of sweat. We could never leave her. Not our Lottie. But you know how it goes. It's the way they do it now. Beds are super expensive. They needed the room, the cords, the oxygen.

My husband's playing Folsom Prison Blues now. It's got a real swing to it and I find myself bopping and tapping at the table. The kettle is rumbling on the bench, ghosts are curling out of the spout and I warm to them. They are seeping out from the walls. I can feel them sticking to the lino, swaying in the corners, breaking my biscuits, switching the iron on and off, on and off. The sound of the boiling water is cathartic. I hear the ghosts' whispers susurrating through the cracks and I swear tomorrow I'm gunna finally find myself a whistling kettle. It's like the sounds saunter out and in and start filling up my empty spaces. Everybody has empty spaces, from people and things, and sometimes they hurt a bit. And sometimes you hate yourself for not being the best you, regretting things you could have done and said differently. And sometimes it takes a whole army of ghosts and glitter and tea and biscuits, sometimes even buying a house, to really start filling those voids.

Ever since I bought my Nan and Lottie's house, I've heard whistling and whispers and my empty spaces are filling up with the sounds. All day, I've stuck to this gleaming lino floor, no matter what shoes I wear. But maybe that's what happens when you become an adult, your empty spaces start filling up and your memories stick to you. They all stick to you like whistles and shiny lino, and make you glow.

ACKNOWLEDGMENTS

I'd like to pass on my thanks to Sam Mills, Andrea Johnson, Darcy Tranter-Cook, Kyra Bandte, Lisa Ballantyne, my family, the music of Daniel Champagne, and the super communities of Pambula, Eden and Merimbula. A big thanks also goes out to Bridget Lutherborrow, Jess Magrath and Bronwyn Mehan, from Spineless Wonders.

The Waterfowl Are Drunk! was first released by Spineless Wonders as part of its Slinkies Under 30s series, a platform for emerging writers. This digital series was curated and edited by writer, academic and editor, Bridget Lutherborrow. Bridget is currently writing a novel about lumberjills and a thesis about weird narration as part of a PhD at the University of Wollongong. Her short story collection *Thirteen Story Horse* was published in 2015 by Going Down Swinging.

shortaustralianstories.com.au

CPSIA information can be obtained
at www.ICGtesting.com
Printed in the USA
BVOW10s0322151116
4847BVAU00005B/2/P